Stopwatch books

(All books are in hardback unless indicated otherwise.)

Apple tree
Birds' nest (pbk only)
Broad bean (pbk only)
Bumblebee (pbk only)
Butterfly and caterpillar
Chicken and egg
Conker
Dandelion
Dragonfly
Earwig
Fly
Hamster (pbk only)
Honeybee
House mouse

Hyacinth
Ladybird
Mosquito
Moth
Mushroom
Newt
Potato
Snail (pbk only)
Spider's web (pbk only)
Stickleback
Strawberry
Tadpole and frog
Tomato

888797

595.4

First paperback edition 1991

First published 1984 in hardback by
A & C Black (Publishers) Limited
35 Bedford Row, London WC1R 4JH

ISBN 0–7136–3499–5

Copyright © 1991, 1984 A & C Black (Publishers) Ltd

A CIP catalogue record for this book
is available from the British Library.

Acknowledgements
The artwork is by B L Kearley Ltd

Filmset by August Filmsetting, Haydock, St Helens
Printed in Belgium by Proost International Book Production

Spider's web

Christine Back
Photographs by Barrie Watts

Adam and Charles Black · London

The spider is going to make a web.

This book tells you how a garden spider spins its web.

Here is a female spider starting her web. First she spins a thread. The spider sticks one end of the thread to a twig. She lets the other end flutter in the wind. Soon this end sticks on to a leaf.

Now the thread is stretched between a twig and a leaf. It looks like this.

Look at the photograph. The thread is very thin, so you cannot see all of it. But it is very strong.

The thread comes out of the spider's body.

Look at this photograph.

At the end of the spider's body, there are six tiny tubes.
Can you see them? The tubes are called spinnerets.
The thread comes out of the spinnerets.

Look at the big photograph. You can see the spider
pulling a thread out of her body. The spider uses
two legs to pull out the thread. She holds on to the
web with her other legs.

The spider makes a frame for her web.

The spider spins some more threads. She fastens each
thread to a twig or leaf. These threads will be
the outside of the web.

Next, the spider spins some threads which look like
the spokes of a wheel.
Now the web looks like this.

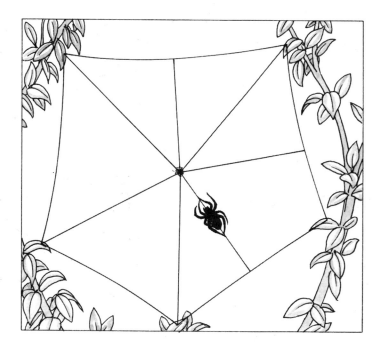

Look at the photograph. Can you see two threads which
look like the spokes of a wheel?

The spider makes the web stronger.

In the middle of the web, the spider spins a spiral of thread.
Now the web looks like this.

Look at the photograph. Can you see the spiral of
thread in the middle of the web?

The spider spins special sticky threads.

The spider starts to spin new threads. She goes around the edge of the web, like this.

The new part of the web is made from special sticky threads.

Look at the photograph. Can you see the blobs of sticky stuff on the threads? What do you think they are for?

The spider keeps spinning more sticky threads.

The spider gets nearer and nearer to the middle of the web.

Look at this drawing.

When the spider gets near to the middle of the web, she eats the spiral of thread which she made there before. This makes room for more sticky threads.

Look at the photograph. Can you see the spider in the middle of the web? She is eating the threads there.

The spider's web is finished.

Look at the drawing.

You can see all the threads in the web.

Now look at the photograph. The sticky threads show up best.

A web this shape is called an orb web. Spider's webs are not all the same shape as this one. Different kinds of spiders make different shaped webs.

The spider waits near the web.

The spider has made her web for catching food.
She will eat any insects which fly into the web.

The spider hides near the web. She keeps hold of a thin
thread which is joined to the web. If something flies
into the web, the spider will feel the thread move.

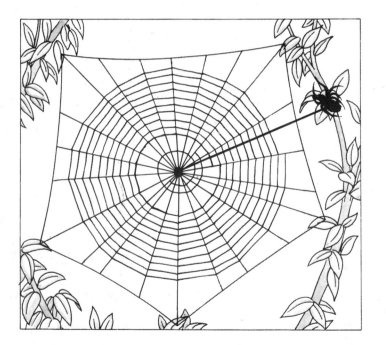

Look at the photograph. Can you see the spider
holding the thread?

An insect gets caught in the web.

The spider doesn't have to wait very long. A crane-fly flies into the web and gets caught on the sticky threads. Look at the photograph. The crane-fly is tearing the web as it tries to get away.

Now look at the drawing.

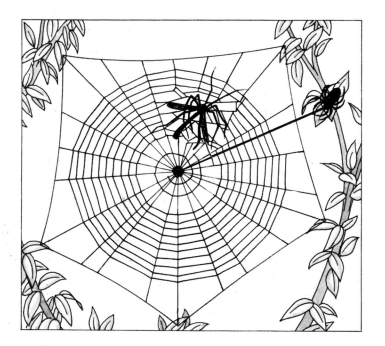

The spider feels the web move. She knows that there is food in the web.

The spider wraps the insect in thread.

The spider goes on to the web. She bites the crane-fly with her fangs. This puts poison into the crane-fly's body.

Now the crane-fly stops struggling. It is still alive but it cannot move. The spider wraps the crane-fly in silk thread.

Look at the photograph. Can you see the crane-fly inside the parcel of thread? It will stay there until the spider is ready to eat.

The spider eats the insect.

The spider is hungry. She carries the crane-fly to the middle of the web. Then the spider begins to eat. She sucks all the juices out of the crane-fly and leaves the hard outer-skin behind.

When the spider has finished eating, she has a rest.

Later, she will start to make a new web.
Then what do you think will happen?

Do you remember how the spider makes her web?
See if you can tell the story in your own words.
You can use these pictures to help you.

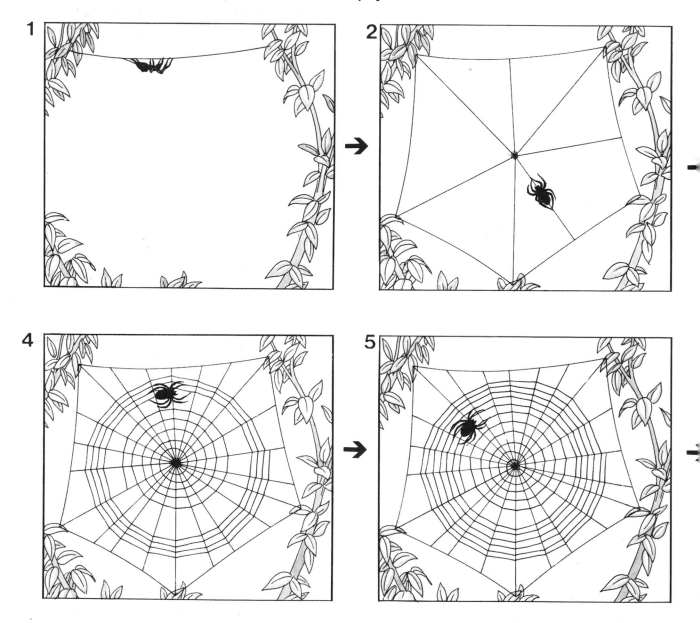

Index

This index will help you to find some of the important words in the book.

Now look out for spider's webs in parks and gardens. You might see a spider building its web, or an insect caught in the web.